PROFESSOR VON VOLT IS A FAMOUS SCIENTIST. HE DESIGNED THIS TIME MACHINE FOR THE STILTON FAMILY: THEIR MISSION IS TO DEFEAT THE PIRATE CATS AND SAVE HISTORY!

SPEEDRAT

Geronimo Stilton

THE SECRET
OF THE SPHINX

PAPERCUTZ™

Geronimo Stilton & Thea Stilton

GRAPHIC NOVELS AVAILABLE FROM PAPERCUTZ
...ALSO AVAILABLE WHEREVER E-BOOKS ARE SOLD!

#1 "The Discovery of America" #2 "The Secret of the Sphinx" #3 "The Coliseum Con" #4 "Following the Trail of Marco Polo" #5 "The Great Ice Age" #6 "Who Stole The Mona Lisa?"

#7 "Dinosaurs in Action" #8 "Play It Again, Mozart!" #9 "The Weird Book Machine" #10 "Geronimo Stilton Saves the Olympics" #11 "We'll Always Have Paris" #12 "The First Samurai"

#13 "The Fastest Train in the West" #14 "The First Mouse on the Moon" #15 "All for Stilton, Stilton for All!" #16 "Lights, Camera, Stilton!"

#1 "The Secret of Whale Island" #2 "Revenge of the Lizard Club" #3 "The Treasure of the Viking Ship" #4 "Catching the Giant Wave"

papercutz.com

Geronimo Stilton

THE SECRET OF THE SPHINX

By Geronimo Stilton

New York

THE SECRET OF THE SPHINX
© EDIZIONI PIEMME 2007, S.p.A.
Via Tiziano 32, 20145
Milan, Italy

Text by Geronimo Stilton
Based on an original idea by Elisabetta Dami
Editorial coordination by Patrizia Puricelli
Original editing by Daniela Finistauri
Script by Demetrio Bargellini
Artistic coordination by Roberta Bianchi
Artistic assistance by Tommaso Valsecchi
Graphic Project by Michela Battaglin
Graphics by Sara Baruffaldi and Marta Lorini
Cover art and color by Flavio Ferron
Interior illustrations by Gianluigi Fungo
Coloring by Mirko Babboni

Historical Advisory on Ancient Egypt by Dr. Marcella Trapani, Piedmont Department
of Archeological Heritage and the Egyptian Museum of Turin
© 2009 – for this work in English language by Papercutz.

Original title: Geronimo Stilton Il Segreto Della Sfinge
Translation by: Nanette McGuinness

www.geronimostilton.com

Lettering and Production by Big Bird Zatryb
Michael Petranek – Associate Editor
Beth Scorzato– Production Coordinator
Jim Salicrup
Editor-in-Chief

ISBN: 978-1-59707-159-8

Printed in China
March 2016 by WKT CO LTD
3/F Leader Industrial Centre
188 Texaco Road
Tsuen Wan, N.T.

Distributed by Macmillan.
Twelfth Papercutz Printing

THE SECRET OF THE SPHINX

IT ALL BEGAN ON A VERY COLD WINTER MORNING. NEW MOUSE CITY HAD BEEN PARALYZED BY A THREE FOOT BLANKET OF SNOW FOR DAYS...

...AND I WAS STAYING IN THE COZY WARMTH OF MY HOUSE, FULLY DRESSED, TO KEEP MY *WHISKERS FROM FREEZING!*

BUT HOW CARELESS OF ME! I'VE FORGOTTEN TO INTRODUCE MYSELF: MY NAME IS STILTON, GERONIMO STILTON! AND I EDIT THE RODENT'S GAZETTE, THE MOST FAMOUSE PAPER ON MOUSE ISLAND!

-BRRR!-

SO I WAS STAYING IN THE WARMTH WHEN THE DOORBELL RANG!

RIIING

?!?

WHO KNOWS WHO IT COULD BE IN THIS MISERABLE WEATHER...

5

MOLDY MOZZARELLA! I'M COMING, I'M COMING!

RIIING RIIING

WHO IS IT?

STRANGE -- I DON'T SEE ANYONE, EXCEPT FOR THIS SNOWMAN...

HMM... MAYBE I DREAMED I HEARD THE DOORBELL!

-SQUEEEAK!-

SSSS

POW

HA, HA, HA... LIKE THE TRICK, COUSIN? COME ON, LET'S HAVE A SNOWBALL FIGHT!

-SIGH-
I SHOULD'VE GUESSED... TRAP!

COME ON, OKAY? I CAN'T PLAY BY MYSELF!

YOU KNOW I DON'T LIKE SNOW VERY MUCH AND WINTER EVEN LESS!

WINTER?

-TSK-... YOU, MY DEAR GERONIMO, DON'T LIKE ANY SEASON!

"IN SPRING, THERE'S TOO MUCH **WIND**."

"IN SUMMER, IT'S TOO **HOT** AND HUMID."

"IN THE FALL, THERE ARE TOO MANY **LEAVES** ON THE GROUND."

WELL, IF YOU DON'T WANT TO PLAY... YOU CAN ALWAYS OFFER ME A CUP OF HOT CHOCOLATE!

IF THAT'S WHAT YOU WANT, JUST COME INTO THE HOUSE... ~BRRRRR!~

VROOOMM

YOO-HOO! CIAO, G! HI, TRAP!

?!?

P-PETUNIA?

SKREEE

VROOOMM

HELLO, UNCLE TRAP!

HI, KIDS! ARE YOU GOING SOMEPLACE NICE?

THE SCHOOLS ARE CLOSED, SO I'M TAKING BENJAMIN AND BUGSY FOR A RIDE ON MY NEW SNOW-MOBILE! I WANTED TO ASK G IF--

SPEAKING OF HIM, WHERE'D HE GO?

GERONIMO? HE WAS HERE JUST A MOMENT AGO!

UH-OH!

RUN INTO THE HOUSE AND LOOK FOR A SHOVEL!

I'LL HELP YOU!

OUR GERONIMO ISN'T HAPPY IF HE'S NOT IN A JAM!

INDEED! HE ALWAYS MANAGES TO GET HIMSELF INTO A FIX!

ATTENTION! ATTENTION! A MESSAGE FOR THE STILTON FAMILY!

HUH?

CALAMITOUS CATS! THAT SNOWMAN TALKS!

I REPEAT, A MESSAGE FOR THE STILTON FAMILY!

HEY! I KNOW THAT *VOICE!*

SQUEAK!

PROFESSOR VON VOLT! IS THAT YOU?

AH, GOOD MORNING, MISS PRETTY PAWS!

SORRY FOR GETTING IN TOUCH WITH YOU IN THIS **BIZARRE** WAY, BUT THE CITY IS COMPLETELY BLOCKED BY SNOW AND PUTTING A TV CAMERA AND A TRANSCEIVER INTO A SNOWMAN...

...SEEMED LIKE THE EASIEST WAY TO CONTACT GERONIMO!

YOU'RE REALLY A **GENIUS**, PROFESSOR!

THANKS! I NEED TO SEE GERONIMO AND YOU ALL URGENTLY!

WHERE ARE YOU, PROFESSOR?

I'LL GIVE YOU THE DIRECTIONS TO MY SECRET LABORATORY RIGHT NOW! BUT I DON'T SEE GERONIMO: WHERE IS HE?

UM, AT THE MOMENT HE'S... OCCUPIED!

ONCE AT PROFESSOR VON VOLT'S LAB...

WE'RE HERE, PROFESSOR!

SORRY FOR THE DELAY, BUT WE RAN INTO SOME **DIFFICULTIES!**

!?

BY THE BONES OF A WERECAT! WHAT HAPPENED TO POOR GERONIMO?

IT'S A LONG STORY! ANYHOW, WE JUST NEED TO WARM HIM UP A BIT...

IN THAT CASE, I'VE GOT SOMETHING THAT WILL DO THE TRICK... A SOLAR *ENERGY LAMP* FOR MELTING METAL!

OH, THAT'S PERFECT, PROFESSOR!

SWIIISH

HANG IN THERE, COUSIN! YOU'LL BE FREE IN A FEW MINUTES...

BZZZ

WHY DID YOU WANT TO SEE US, PROFESSOR?

HUH?

AH, YES... IT'S BECAUSE OF THE TEMPOGRAPH, THE INSTRUMENT I INVENTED TO KEEP AN EYE ON THE PAST! EVER SINCE THIS MORNING, THE DISPLAY HAS BEEN INDICATING A CHANGE... SOMEONE IS TRYING TO CHANGE HISTORY!

OH, NO! THAT MEANS THE PIRATE CATS ARE BACK IN ACTION, RIGHT?

THOSE NASTY CATS!

EXACTLY! THEY'RE TIME-TRAVELING AGAIN AND, KNOWING THEM, THEIR JOURNEY CAN ONLY HAVE ONE GOAL...

...CHANGING HISTORY TO BENEFIT THEM!

THEN WE HAVE TO LEAVE IMMEDIATELY!

WHERE ARE THE PIRATE CATS HEADED?

TO MEMPHIS, THE CAPITOL OF **ANCIENT EGYPT**, IN THE YEAR 2484 B.C., DURING THE REIGN OF THE FOURTH DYNASTY PHARAOH, CHEPHREN!

DO YOU HAVE ANY IDEA WHY THE CATS CHOSE THIS TIME PERIOD?

ONLY SOME SUSPICIONS, MISS PRETTY PAWS!

CHEPHREN BUILT A LARGE PYRAMID. BUT MORE THAN THAT, ACCORDING TO SOME SCHOLARS HE ALSO FINISHED ONE OF THE MOST FAMOUS MONUMENTS IN HISTORY: THE SPHINX!

THE SPHINX HAS THE BODY OF A LION AND THE HEAD OF A MAN. ACCORDING TO SOME SCHOLARS, ITS FACE REPRESENTED THAT OF THE PHARAOH CHEPHREN. 187 FEET LONG AND 65.7 FEET HIGH, IT'S CARVED FROM A SINGLE STONE, AND WAS ORIGINALLY PAINTED IN COLOR.

WHATEVER THE CATS' GOAL MAY BE, WE'LL ONLY DISCOVER IT BY GOING THERE. HURRY UP, GUYS. LET'S GO!

HURRAY! ANOTHER JOURNEY INTO HISTORY!

YEOOWWW! IT'S BURNING! IT'S BURN-ING!

WELCOME BACK, GERONIMO!

?!!

WAIT, I'LL HELP YOU PUT OUT YOUR TAIL!

~:EEEPP!:~

STOMP

BENJAMIN? PROFESSOR VON VOLT?

UNCLE GERONIMO!

GERONIMO, ARE YOU ALL RIGHT?

I'M FINE! BUT WHAT AM I DOING IN PROFESSOR VON VOLT'S LAB?

THERE'S NO TIME TO EXPLAIN! I'LL TELL YOU EVERYTHING ON THE WAY!

ON THE WAY? WHAT WAY? I CAN'T LEAVE, I HAVE A NEWSPAPER TO RUN!

MOLDY MOZZARELLA! I CAN'T LEEEAVE!

GET MOVINGGGG!

?

UM... DON'T FORGET MY SPECIAL EARPIECES THAT LET YOU SPEAK AND UNDERSTAND THE LANGUAGE FROM THAT TIME!

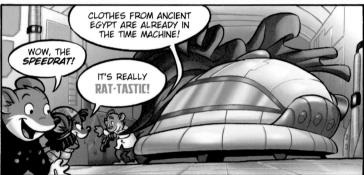

CLOTHES FROM ANCIENT EGYPT ARE ALREADY IN THE TIME MACHINE!

WOW, THE SPEEDRAT!

IT'S REALLY RAT-TASTIC!

BE SURE TO TAKE CARE OF THIS SITUATION, BECAUSE IF THE PIRATE CATS ALTER THE PAST, THEY'LL ALSO CHANGE THE PRESENT -- AND THAT MUST NEVER HAPPEN!

DON'T WORRY, PROFESSOR, WE'LL STOP THE PIRATE CATS! ⋗ SOB ⋖ GOODBYE, PROFESSOR...

⋗ SOB ⋖ GOODBYE, PROFESSOR...

FASTEN YOUR SEAT BELTS!

WAIT A MINUTE, PETUNIA... I'VE CHANGED MY MIND... IT'S BETTER IF I STAY HOME...

ZZIIIP

FROOM

GOOD LUCK, MY FRIENDS!

ZZZAAP

THAT'S THE WAY WE WERE CATAPULTED INTO THE PAST... DESTINATION: ANCIENT EGYPT!

MEANWHILE, AT THE GATES OF MEMPHIS, IN ANCIENT EGYPT...

HURRY UP AND COVER THE SHIP WITH SAND, BONZO!

EGYPTIAN CIVILIZATION
IN 3000 BC, THE LEGENDARY KING, MENES, UNIFIED ALL THE TRIBES THAT HAD UP TO THEN LIVED SEPARATELY FROM EACH OTHER ALONG THE BANKS OF THE NILE RIVER AND SO BEGAN THE FIRST OF THE THIRTY DYNASTIES OF PHARAOHS. FROM THEN ON, EGYPTIAN CIVILIZATION DEVELOPED UNTIL IT REACHED A VERY HIGH LEVEL OF KNOWLEDGE: IT WAS REALLY THE EGYPTIANS WHO CREATED ONE OF THE FIRST FORMS OF WRITING. IN ADDITION, THEY DEVOTED THEMSELVES TO POETRY, SCULPTURE, ARCHITECTURE, MATHEMATICS AND MEDICINE.

MEMPHIS
FOUNDED AROUND THE END OF THE FOURTH MILLENNIUM BC, THE CITY OF MEMPHIS WAS THE CAPITAL OF EGYPT DURING THE PREDYNASTIC PERIOD (2920-2575 BC) AND THE OLD KINGDOM (2575-2134 BC).

GIZA

MEMPHIS

NILE RIVER

I'M CATARDONE, RULER OF THE PIRATE CATS. I CAN'T GET MY PAWS DIRTY!

⇒ PUFF! PANT! ⇐ SO I HAVE TO DO EVERYTHING BY MYSELF?

CERTAINLY! AS THE LEADER, CATARDONE'S JOB IS... TO THINK!

OF COURSE!

→ *GULP!* ←
TO THINK?
WHAT ABOUT, TERSILLA?

HOW TO REACH OUR GOAL, NATURALLY!

HA, HA, HA... OF COURSE!

SCRITCH SCRITCH

HMMM...

BONZO, LET'S HEAR IF YOU REMEMBER OUR GOAL!

UMM... COVERING THE TIME MACHINE WITH SAND?

THE SPHINX, YOU IDIOT... *THE SPHINX!* WE'RE GOING TO CONVINCE PHARAOH TO GIVE IT THE FACE OF A CAT! THAT WAY WE'LL BE REMEMBERED FOREVER!

AND HOW WILL WE MANAGE TO CONVINCE PHARAOH TO DO THAT?

WE'LL USE OUR TYPICAL CAT *SHREWDNESS!*

YES, I'M SHREWD, VERY SHREWD, VERY, VERY SHREWD!

MEOW... I WASN'T TALKING ABOUT YOU, BONZO!

COME ON! LET'S PUT ON OUR MOUSE MASKS. THEN YOU CAN DRESS UP AS PRIESTS OF THE GODDESS BASTET, THE PATRON GODDESS OF CATS... I'LL BE A TEMPLE DANCER!

DIVINITY
THE ANCIENT EGYPTIANS WORSHIPPED A NUMBER OF DIVINITIES, INCLUDING RA, THE SUN GOD, OSIRIS, THE GOD OF DEATH, HIS WIFE ISIS, THEIR SON HORUS, WHO HAD THE HEAD OF A FALCON, AND BASTET, DAUGHTER OF THE GOD RA. BASTET HAD THE HEAD OF A CAT.

→ *NNNNGGG!* ←

HMPH! MY MASK MUST HAVE SHRUNK OVER THE PAST FEW MONTHS!

NO, DADDY DEAR, YOU'VE PUT ON WEIGHT!

14

THERE, I'M DONE! NO ONE WILL SUSPECT THAT THE *CATJET* IS HIDDEN UNDER THIS SAND MASTERPIECE!

?!

DO YOU WANT TO LET EVERYONE KNOW THAT WE COME FROM THE FUTURE?!? SKYSCRAPERS DON'T EXIST YET HERE!

NO, I...

DESTROY THIS MOUSURDITY!*

⇥SOB!⇤

*ABSURDITY

SO, HALF AN HOUR LATER...

NOW THAT THE CATJET IS WELL HIDDEN AND WE ARE DRESSED LIKE MICE FROM ANCIENT EGYPT, LET'S SWING INTO ACTION!

YES, TERSILLA!

Y-Y-YES, TERSILLA!

HOW COME YOUR DAUGHTER GIVES THE COMMANDS, IF YOU'RE THE BOSS?

HUH?

TERSILLA DOESN'T GIVE COMMANDS! SHE RESTRICTS HERSELF TO JUST EXPRESSING MY THOUGHTS!

⇥SIGH!⇤ WHY DO I HAVE TO PUT UP WITH *DUMMIES* LIKE THESE TWO?!?

A LITTLE LATER, AT THE ROYAL PALACE IN MEMPHIS...

NOBLE VIZIER RAT-KARUE, TWO PRIESTS OF THE GODDESS BASTET ARE REQUESTING AN AUDIENCE!

THE VIZIER
WAS THE PHARAOH'S PRIME MINISTER AND WORKED WITH THE PHARAOH IN DIRECTING NUMEROUS AFFAIRS OF STATE. HE WAS, THEREFORE, IN CHARGE OF CONVEYING THE ORDERS OF THE KING, COLLECTING TAXES, ADMINISTERING JUSTICE, CHECKING ON THE PROGRESS OF PUBLIC PROJECTS AND THE FLOW OF TRANSPORTATION ON THE RIVER.

PRIESTS?
ALL RIGHT, SEND THEM IN!

YES, MY LORD!

WHATEVER THE REASON FOR THEIR VISIT, IT'S BETTER TO TREAT THEM WITH RESPECT AND NOT ANNOY THE GODS.

PRIESTS
IN ANCIENT EGYPT, PRIESTS CELEBRATED THE RELIGIOUS RITES FOR WORSHIPPING THE DIFFERENT DIVINITIES. AS A RESULT, THERE WERE MANY TO KEEP UP WITH AND THEY ENJOYED NUMEROUS PRIVILEGES.

THANK YOU FOR RECEIVING US, OH MOST ILLUSTRIOUS VIZIER! I AM CAT-SINUHE AND THIS IS BON-ZETET. WE ARE PRIESTS OF THE GODDESS BASTET.

I, ON THE OTHER HAND, AM RAT-SHEPSUT, TEMPLE DANCER FOR THE GODDESS BASTET.

TELL ME EVERYTHING! UNFORTUNATELY I CAN ONLY GIVE YOU A LITTLE TIME!

~YAWN!~

THAT WILL BE ENOUGH TIME TO SHOW YOU THE MOST INCREDIBLE **MIRACLE!**

BON-ZETET HAS RECEIVED A GIFT FROM THE GODDESS BASTET.

AND THAT IS? NOT THE APPEARANCE OF INTELLIGENCE, IT SEEMS TO ME!

~ZZ~

ONE NIGHT, BON-ZETET FELL ASLEEP NEXT TO A STATUE OF THE GODDESS BASTET, AND EVER SINCE THEN, WE'VE DISCOVERED THAT THE GODDESS SPEAKS THROUGH HIM...

ALL YOU HAVE TO DO IS STEP ON HIS TAIL... LIKE THIS!

MEOOOWWW!

STOMP

M-M-MEOW?!?

WAIL OF A CAT... EVEN THOUGH HE'S A MOUSE, LIKE US!

THAT WAS THE WAIL OF A CAT... EVEN THOUGH HE'S A MOUSE, LIKE US!

IT'S THE GODDESS BASTET WHO'S SPEAKING!

HMM... HOW CAN I BE SURE THIS ISN'T SOME KIND OF TRICK?

IF YOU DON'T BELIEVE US, MOST ILLUSTRIOUS VIZIER, TRY IT YOURSELF!

YES, MOST ILLUSTRIOUS VIZIER, JUST TREAD ON HIS TAIL!

HEY... JUST A MINUTE!

HMM... THE GODDESS BASTET... WHO SPEAKS...

UH-OH!

NAAAH! IT'S NOT POSSIBLE!

~PHEWWWW!~

!

YANK

17

MEOOOWWWW!

NOW ARE YOU CONVINCED OF THE MIRACLE, MOST ILLUSTRIOUS RAT-KARLIE?

YES. ACTUALLY, I'M CURIOUS TO KNOW WHAT HE'S SAYING!

IT'S BETTER THAT WE DON'T! BUT IF YOU TAKE US IN YOUR SERVICE, OUR DANCER WILL TRANSLATE THE MESSAGES OF THE GODDESS!

AS A MATTER OF FACT, SHE ALONE CAN UNDERSTAND THE WORDS OF THE GODDESS!

REALLY? AND HAS THE GODDESS EVER SPOKEN ABOUT ME?

BUT OF COURSE, *MOST ILLUSTRIOUS VIZIER!* IT WAS ACTUALLY THE GODDESS BASTET WHO ORDERED US TO COME HERE!

SHE SAID, "GO TO MEMPHIS AND TAKE MY ADVISERS TO RAT-KARLIE, VIZIER TO CHEPHREN, A RODENT WHOSE INTELLIGENCE IS GREATER THAN ANYONE ELSE'S!"

EVEN PHARAOH'S?

PHARAOH'S AND THE WHOLE ROYAL FAMILY.

THE GODDESS GAVE YOU A **SPECIAL** GIFT, TOO?

YES, OF COURSE... INTELLIGENCE!

STRANGE... I HADN'T NOTICED THAT!

÷GULP!÷

OKAY, I'LL TAKE YOU INTO MY SERVICE! YOUR ARRIVAL AND THE FAVOR OF BASTET WILL BE A BLESSING FOR ALL OF EGYPT!

YOU WON'T REGRET IT, OH MOST ILLUSTRIOUS VIZIER!

÷SOB!÷ I PREDICT HARD TIMES FOR MY TAIL!

MORE INTELLIGENT THAN PHARAOH CHEPHREN AND THE ROYAL FAMILY! THE GODS HAVE BIG PLANS FOR ME...

WE FINALLY ARRIVED IN **Egypt...**

~>SQUEEAK!<~

CLANG

OOPS... SORRY ABOUT THE LANDING!

~>GROAN<~... I THINK MY *TAIL'S* BRUISED!

HEY! WHERE DID WE END UP?

THE SHIP COMPUTER SAYS WE ARE 11 MILES NORTH OF MEMPHIS!

MOLDY MOZZARELLA! WE LANDED IN THE DESERT!

IT'S LIKELY THERE'S AN ERROR IN THE SHIP COMPUTER FROM WHEN TRAP SUBSTITUTED FOR ME AS DRIVER!

HEY, WHAT'S IT GOT TO DO WITH ME?

YOU'RE THE ONE WHO REPROGRAMMED THE COMPUTER BECAUSE YOU WANTED TO STOP OFF IN THE MIDDLE AGES... FOR A SNACK!

⇢TSK⇠... MAYBE IT HAPPENED WHEN YOU HOPPED AROUND ALL OVER THE PLACE JUST BECAUSE I TICKLED YOU!

IT'S NOT MY FAULT I'M TICKLISH!

THE FACT REMAINS THAT WE NOW FIND OURSELVES IN A DESERT MORE DESERTED THAN THE SAHARA!

!

WELL, MAYBE IT'S NOT QUITE THAT DESERTED! LOOK!

ROTTEN ROQUEFORT! A PYRAMID!

IT'S GIGANTIC!

OF COURSE, WE LANDED ON THE GIZA PLATEAU! THIS HAS TO BE THE PYRAMID OF CHEOPS!

GIZA PLATEAU
NORTH OF MEMPHIS, IT WAS CHOSEN BY THE PHARAOH CHEOPS, CHEPHREN'S FATHER, AS THE SITE FOR HIS OWN PYRAMID. AT 480 FEET IN HEIGHT AND 656 FEET ALONG EACH SIDE AT THE BASE, THE PYRAMID OF CHEOPS IS THE LARGEST PYRAMID IN ANCIENT EGYPT. IT TOOK OVER 20 YEARS TO BUILD AND MORE THAN 2,000,000 BLOCKS OF STONE THAT WEIGHED AROUND 2.5 TONS EACH. THE PYRAMIDS OF CHEPHREN, HIS SON MICERINO, AND THE SPHINX WERE ALSO BUILT AT GIZA.

COME ON! LET'S HIDE THE TIME MACHINE AND GET OURSELVES READY!

AFTER PUTTING ON CLOTHING FROM THAT TIME PERIOD...

DONE! THE SPEEDRAT WON'T ATTRACT ANY PRYING EYES UNDER THIS DUNE!

UNLIKE MY KILT! I FEEL RIDICULOUS, PETUNIA!

GERONIMO YOU'RE *ALWAYS* RIDICULOUS, DON'T YOU KNOW THAT? EVEN WHEN YOU'RE WEARING NORMAL CLOTHES!

THANK YOU, TRAP!

I HOPE WE MEET SOMEONE WE CAN ASK FOR DIRECTIONS. OTHERWISE WE MAY GET LOST!

IT'S SO HOT! I ALMOST MISS THE COLD OF NEW MOUSE CITY!

TELL ME ABOUT IT, BENJAMIN!

HEY! THERE'S A CONSTRUCTION SITE OVER THERE! THEY'RE BUILDING ANOTHER *PYRAMID!*

IT DEFINITELY HAS TO BE CHEPHREN'S. HE'S THE PHARAOH WHO RULED IN THIS ERA!

DID YOU NOTICE, UNCLE G? TO THE RIGHT OF THE PYRAMID IS ANOTHER MONUMENT... BUT IT'S ALL COVERED UP...

THAT HAS TO BE THE SPHINX, WHICH HASN'T BEEN FINISHED YET!

LET'S TURN ON THE EARPIECES PROFESSOR VON VOLT GAVE US AND GET CLOSER!

CLICK

SO WE WENT CLOSER TO THE PYRAMID CONSTRUCTION SITE...

CHIN UP, ONE MORE PUSH! IT'S THE LAST STONE **OF THE DAY!**

~NNNNGGG!~

HELLO! CAN YOU SHOW US THE WAY TO GET TO MEMPHIS?

!?

AND WHO ARE YOU? I'VE NEVER SEEN YOU AT THE SITE BEFORE!

WE'RE VISITORS FROM FAR AWAY! MY NAME IS *ST...GERON-ANKH-AMON!* I'M A SCRIBE!

SCRIBES

IN ANCIENT EGYPT, SCRIBES WERE AMONG THE FEW WHO KNEW HOW TO WRITE. THEY WROTE ON SHEETS OF PAPYRUS, USING PEN NIBS MADE FROM REED OR CANE THAT WERE FIRST SOAKED IN WATER AND THEN DIPPED IN INK.

MY NAME IS RATTY-ATUM AND I'M THE CHIEF ARCHITECT OF THE DIVINE PHARAOH CHEPHREN!

~NNNNNNGG!~

I'M IN CHARGE OF THE WORK ON HIS PYRAMID!

SNAP

22

RRUUUMBLE

-SQUEEEAK!-

THESE ARE MY FRIENDS PET-NEFRET, MY COUSIN RAT-TRAP, MY NEPHEW BEN-JA-PET AND HIS FRIEND BUG-SI-WUG...

WATCH OUT! THE STONE, THE STONE!

BY THE EYES OF RA!

RRUUUMBLE

FLEA-BITTEN WERECAT FUR!

ZOOM

QUICK, MOVE AWAY!

SLAM

WHAT WAS THAT?

I-I-I'M OKAY!

ARE YOU ALL RIGHT, KIDS?

YES, BUT--WAIT A MINUTE! WHERE IS UNCLE GERON-ANKH-AMON?

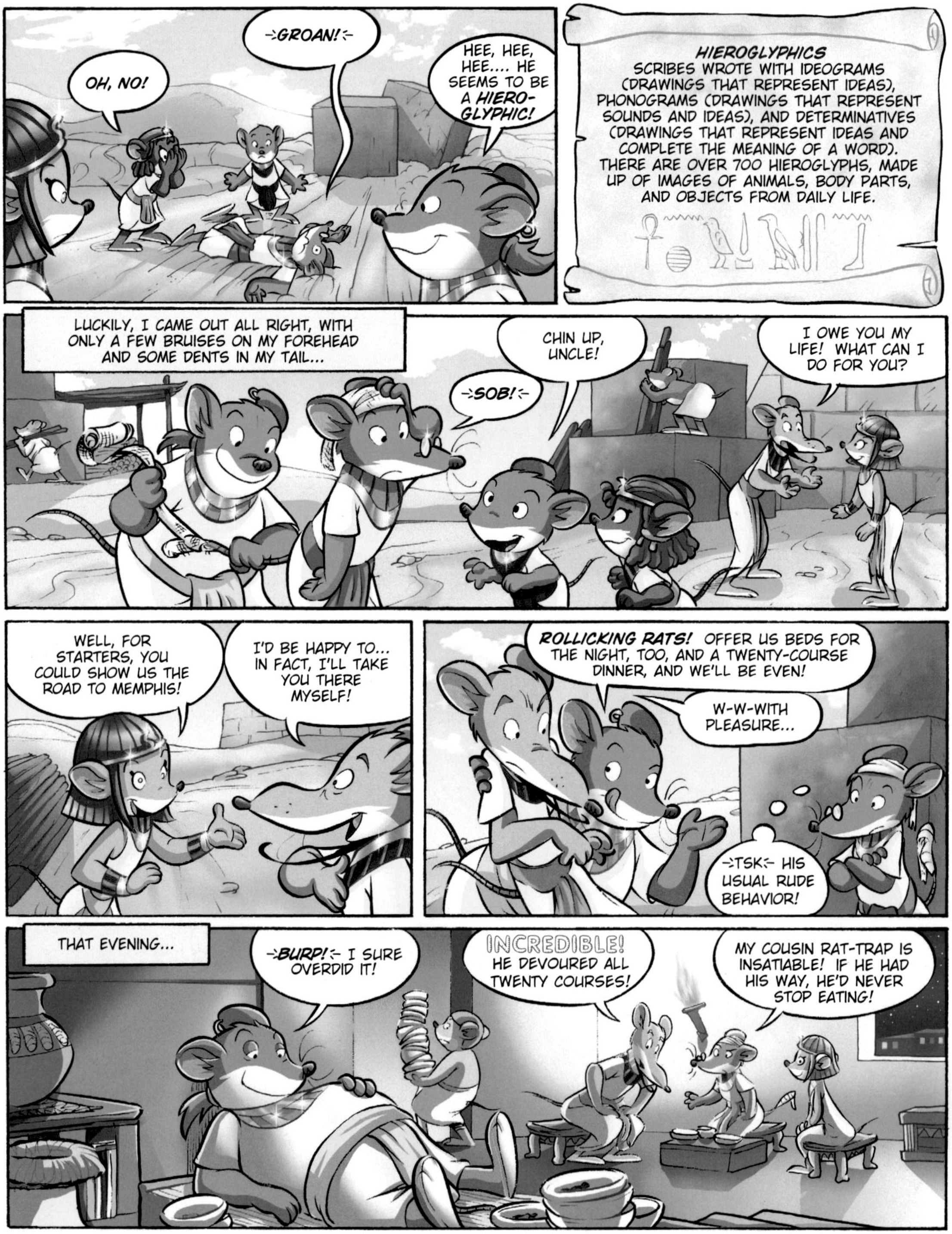
OH, NO!
-GROAN!-
HEE, HEE, HEE.... HE SEEMS TO BE A HIERO-GLYPHIC!
HIEROGLYPHICS
SCRIBES WROTE WITH IDEOGRAMS (DRAWINGS THAT REPRESENT IDEAS), PHONOGRAMS (DRAWINGS THAT REPRESENT SOUNDS AND IDEAS), AND DETERMINATIVES (DRAWINGS THAT REPRESENT IDEAS AND COMPLETE THE MEANING OF A WORD). THERE ARE OVER 700 HIEROGLYPHS, MADE UP OF IMAGES OF ANIMALS, BODY PARTS, AND OBJECTS FROM DAILY LIFE.
LUCKILY, I CAME OUT ALL RIGHT, WITH ONLY A FEW BRUISES ON MY FOREHEAD AND SOME DENTS IN MY TAIL...
-SOB!-
CHIN UP, UNCLE!
I OWE YOU MY LIFE! WHAT CAN I DO FOR YOU?
WELL, FOR STARTERS, YOU COULD SHOW US THE ROAD TO MEMPHIS!
I'D BE HAPPY TO... IN FACT, I'LL TAKE YOU THERE MYSELF!
ROLLICKING RATS! OFFER US BEDS FOR THE NIGHT, TOO, AND A TWENTY-COURSE DINNER, AND WE'LL BE EVEN!
W-W-WITH PLEASURE...
-TSK- HIS USUAL RUDE BEHAVIOR!
THAT EVENING...
-BURP!- I SURE OVERDID IT!
INCREDIBLE! HE DEVOURED ALL TWENTY COURSES!
MY COUSIN RAT-TRAP IS INSATIABLE! IF HE HAD HIS WAY, HE'D NEVER STOP EATING!

ON THE OTHER HAND, THE KIDS BARELY TOUCHED THEIR DINNER!

POOR LITTLE MOUSELINGS, THEY WERE SO TIRED THAT THEY FELL RIGHT ASLEEP!

-ZZZ-

SO TELL ME, FRIEND, WHAT BRINGS YOU TO MEMPHIS?

WELL, NOW...

WE'RE HERE TO VISIT THE capitol!

UMM... EXACTLY!

WHAT A SPLENDID IDEA!

IF YOU'LL PERMIT ME, I'LL BE YOUR GUIDE... I COULD TAKE YOU TO VISIT THE ROYAL PALACE!

THE ROYAL PALACE?

OF COURSE! THE PHARAOH WILL BE HAPPY TO MEET THE RODENTS WHO SAVED MY LIFE!

YOU'RE VERY KIND, RATTY-ATUM, BUT WE DON'T WANT TO BOTHER YOU!

THEY SAY THE COURT OF CHEPHREN IS LUXURIOUS IS IT?

IT'S AT LEAST A BIT PHARAOH-NICAL ...AND EVER SINCE THE TWO PRIESTS AND DANCER OF THE GODDESS BASTET ARRIVED...

...IT'S GOTTEN MORE LUXURIOUS!

???

VIZIER RAT-KARUE DOES EVERYTHING THOSE PRIESTS ORDER AND DRAWS FROM THE ROYAL COFFERS TO SATISFY THEIR EVERY REQUEST!

25

"THEY ASKED FOR SOLID GOLD STATUES OF CATS AND THE GODDESS BASTET.."

"...AND OFFERED THE GODDESS BASTET FRESH FISH DELIVERED DAILY FROM THE COAST..."

WHAT'S MORE, THEY EVEN WANTED TO DEDICATE THAT GIGANTIC MONUMENT NEAR CHEPHREN'S PYRAMID TO THE GODDESS!

THE ONE THAT HAS THE BODY OF AN ANIMAL BUT NO FACE CARVED YET?

THAT'S THE SPHINX!

EXACTLY! ACCORDING TO THE PRIESTS, IT SHOULD HAVE THE HEAD OF A CAT RATHER THAN PHARAOH'S FACE!

WHAAAAAAT?

HORRIFYING, DON'T YOU THINK?

HMM... THE HEAD OF A CAT... I SMELL THE *STINK* OF THE PIRATE CATS!

RIGHT, IT CAN'T BE A COINCIDENCE!

BUT I DIDN'T SEE ANY WORK BEING DONE ON THE NEW MONUMENT!

NO, ACTUALLY, WORK HAS STOPPED...

THERE'S BEEN A *DISPUTE* BETWEEN THE PHARAOH AND THE VIZIER! THE PROBLEM IS REALLY ABOUT FINISHING THE FACE...

"ONE DAY, I SAT IN ON ONE OF THEIR DISCUSSIONS ABOUT IT..."

I DEMAND THAT THE MONUMENT WITH THE BODY OF A LION SACRED TO US HAVE MY FACE!

ANIMALS
IN THE ANCIENT EGYPTIAN RELIGION, SOME ANIMALS WERE CONSIDERED SACRED, INCLUDING CATS, CROCODILES, FALCONS, SNAKES, LIONS, AND JACKALS. SCRIBES ALSO USED THE IMAGES OF ANIMALS AS SIGNS FOR WRITING.

BUT, DIVINE PHARAOH, IT'S BASTET WHO HAS ASKED THAT IT HAVE THE FACE OF A CAT. IF WE DON'T CARRY OUT HER COMMANDS, THE GODDESS MAY AVENGE HERSELF ON US!

I'M THE SON OF THE SUN! I'M ALSO A GOD! THE GODDESS BASTET WILL UNDERSTAND MY REASONS!

PHARAOH
ANCIENT EGYPTIANS BELIEVED THAT THE PHARAOH WAS THE HUMAN INCARNATION OF THE GOD HORUS, A GOD WITH THE HEAD OF A FALCON AND THE SON OF THE SUN GOD.

WHICH THE VIZIER DIDN'T DARE ANSWER BACK TO! ANYHOW, FOR THE MOMENT, THE PROJECT IS BLOCKED!

THANK GOODNESS!

OH, BUT I'VE BEEN BORING YOU WITH ALL MY CHATTERING! I'LL BET YOU'RE ALL WORN OUT FROM YOUR JOURNEY!

AS A MATTER OF FACT, IT FEELS LIKE THE JOURNEY TOOK CENTURIES!

MORE THAN CENTURIES... *MILLENNIA!*

YOU'D DO WELL TO FOLLOW THE EXAMPLE OF YOUR FRIENDS AND GET SOME REST! WE HAVE A BIG DAY AHEAD OF US TOMORROW!

÷SNORE, SNORE!÷

SNORE SNORE

SNORE

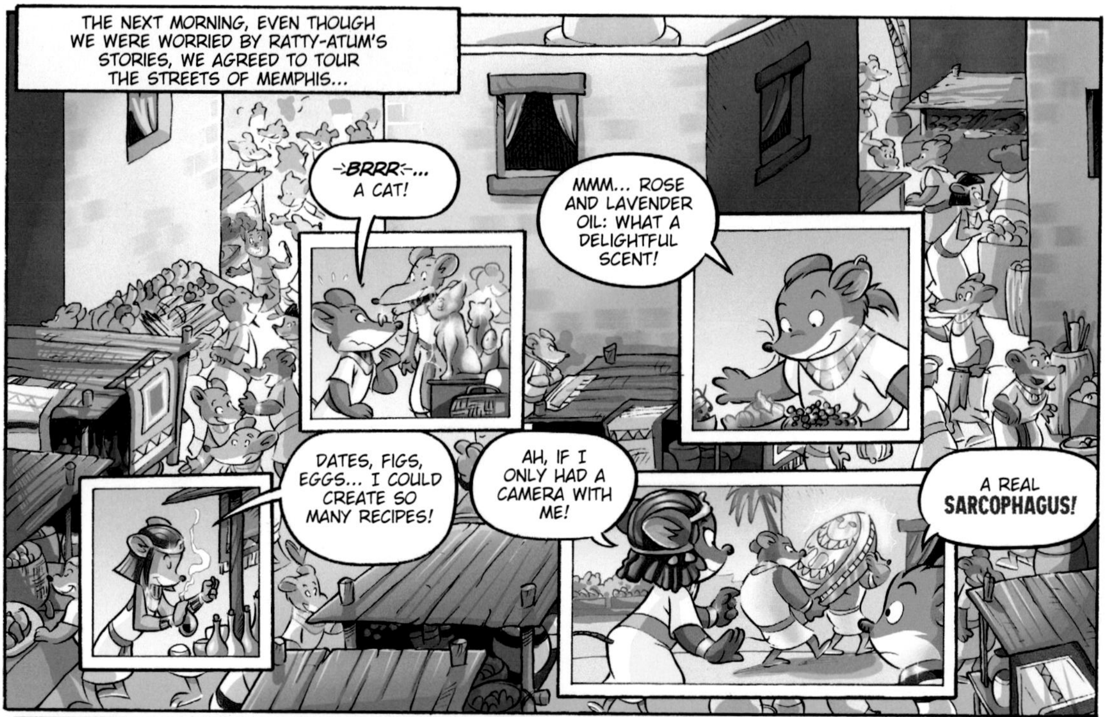
THE NEXT MORNING, EVEN THOUGH WE WERE WORRIED BY RATTY-ATUM'S STORIES, WE AGREED TO TOUR THE STREETS OF MEMPHIS...
BRRR... A CAT!
MMM... ROSE AND LAVENDER OIL: WHAT A DELIGHTFUL SCENT!
DATES, FIGS, EGGS... I COULD CREATE SO MANY RECIPES!
AH, IF I ONLY HAD A CAMERA WITH ME!
A REAL SARCOPHAGUS!

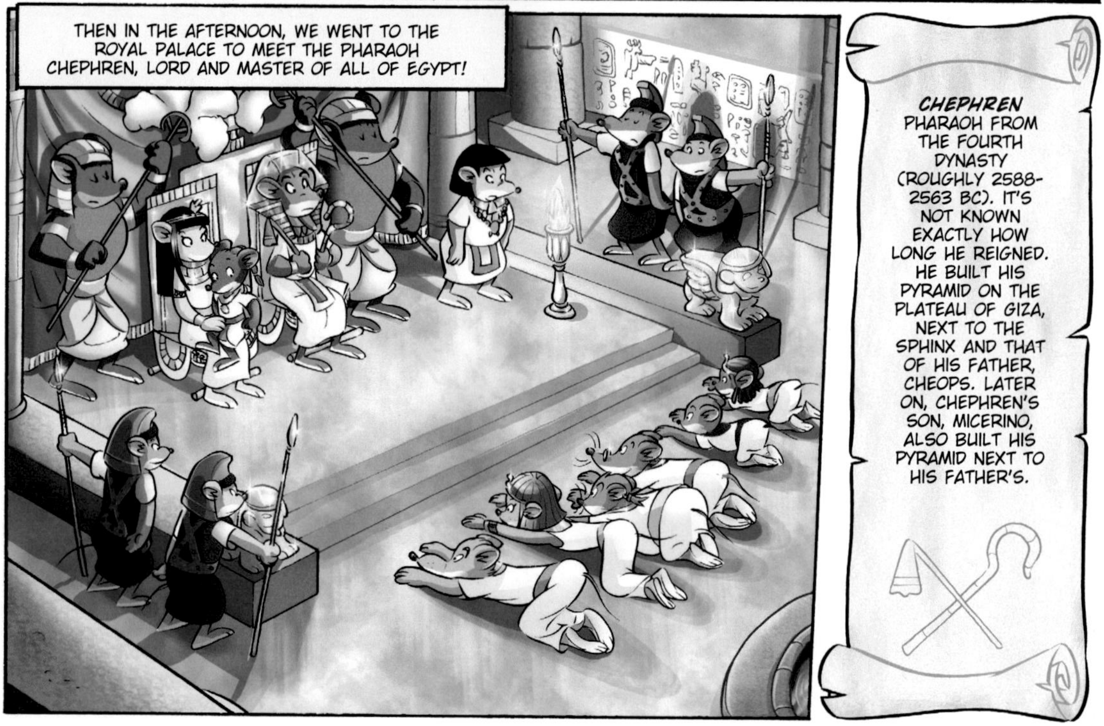
THEN IN THE AFTERNOON, WE WENT TO THE ROYAL PALACE TO MEET THE PHARAOH CHEPHREN, LORD AND MASTER OF ALL OF EGYPT!
CHEPHREN
PHARAOH FROM THE FOURTH DYNASTY (ROUGHLY 2588-2563 BC). IT'S NOT KNOWN EXACTLY HOW LONG HE REIGNED. HE BUILT HIS PYRAMID ON THE PLATEAU OF GIZA, NEXT TO THE SPHINX AND THAT OF HIS FATHER, CHEOPS. LATER ON, CHEPHREN'S SON, MICERINO, ALSO BUILT HIS PYRAMID NEXT TO HIS FATHER'S.

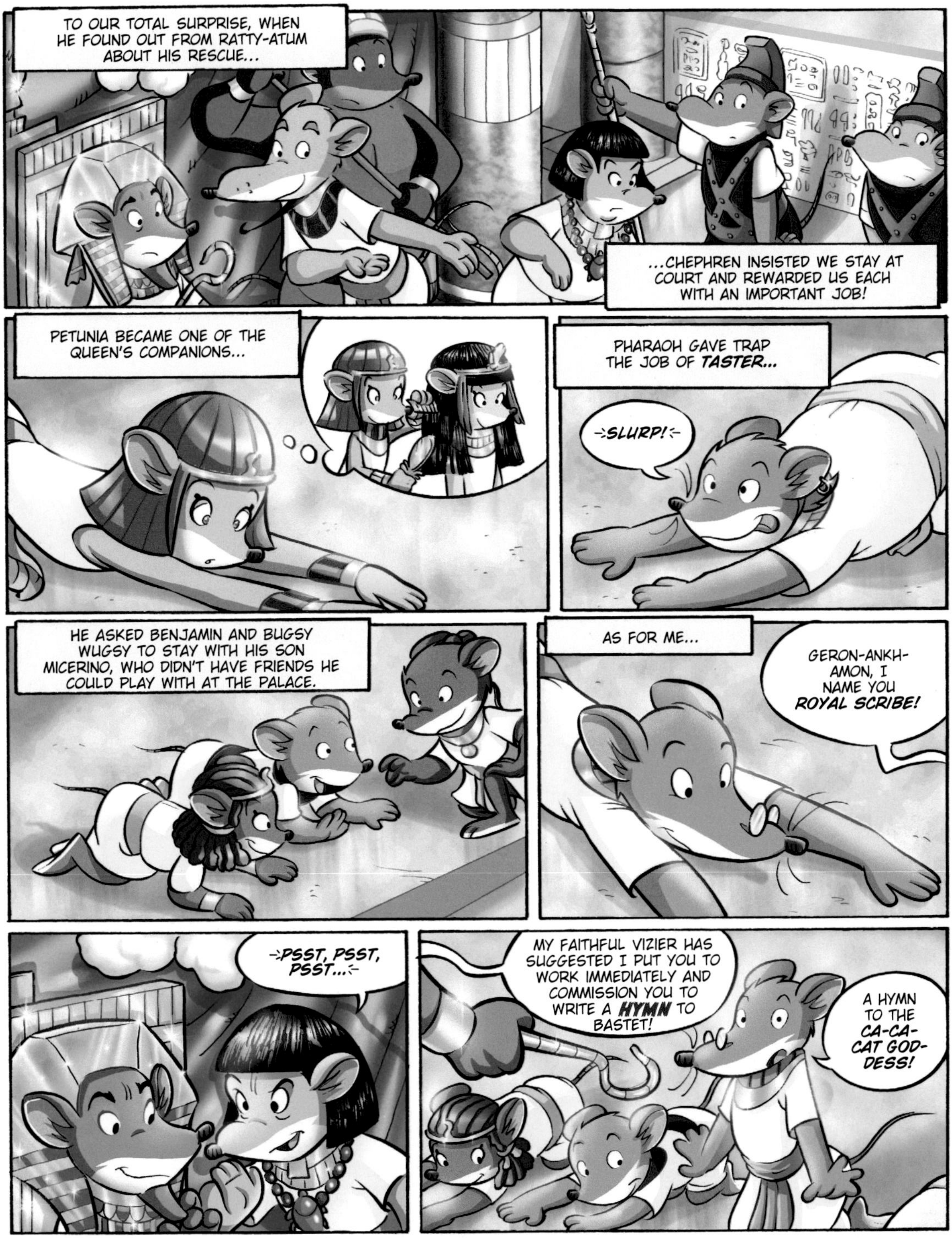
TO OUR TOTAL SURPRISE, WHEN HE FOUND OUT FROM RATTY-ATUM ABOUT HIS RESCUE...
...CHEPHREN INSISTED WE STAY AT COURT AND REWARDED US EACH WITH AN IMPORTANT JOB!
PETUNIA BECAME ONE OF THE QUEEN'S COMPANIONS...
PHARAOH GAVE TRAP THE JOB OF TASTER...
SLURP!
HE ASKED BENJAMIN AND BUGSY WUGSY TO STAY WITH HIS SON MICERINO, WHO DIDN'T HAVE FRIENDS HE COULD PLAY WITH AT THE PALACE.
AS FOR ME...
GERON-ANKH-AMON, I NAME YOU ROYAL SCRIBE!
PSST, PSST, PSST...
MY FAITHFUL VIZIER HAS SUGGESTED I PUT YOU TO WORK IMMEDIATELY AND COMMISSION YOU TO WRITE A HYMN TO BASTET!
A HYMN TO THE CA-CA-CAT GOD-DESS!

SPEAKING OF BASTET, WHERE ARE THE PRIESTS?

I'LL HAVE THEM SUMMONED, OH, DIVINE ONE!

A LITTLE LATER...

HIS EXCELLENCIES CAT-SINUHE AND BON-ZETET, AND THE DANCER RAT-SHEPSUT!

I WOULD LIKE TO INTRODUCE YOU TO MY NEW GUESTS!

?!

~GULP!~ GERONIMO STILTON AND HIS FRIENDS?

~GULP!~ THAT'S GE-GE-GE...

!

MEOOOWWW!

BAM

MEOW?!?

BOW DOWN! THE GREAT GODDESS BASTET HAS SPOKEN!

DON'T KEEP US GUESSING, RAT-SHEPSUT... ONLY YOU CAN TRANSLATE THE WORDS OF THE GODDESS BASTET!

?!?

AS ALWAYS, BASTET WISHES THE PHARAOH A LONG LIFE! IN ADDITION, SHE SENDS A WARM GREETING TO HIS NEW FRIENDS!

EXCELLENT! THANK HER FOR HER **PRECIOUS WORDS!**

GERON-ANKH-AMON, I WANT THE HYMN FOR THE GODDESS BASTET TO BE READY BY NEXT WEEK, FOR THE FESTIVAL IN HONOR OF MY ANNUAL VOYAGE DOWN THE NILE RIVER!

UMM, AT YOUR ORDERS, DIVINE PHARAOH!

GOOD, NOW MY SERVANTS WILL SEE YOU AND YOUR FRIENDS TO YOUR ROOMS!

WE THANKED RATTY-ATUM, PROMISING TO SEE HIM AGAIN SOON, AND THEN WENT TO OUR ROOMS.

PETUNIA AND I TOLD EVERYONE WHAT WE'D REALIZED ABOUT THE SPHINX AND ITS CONSTRUCTION, AND THEN WE GOT TO THE HEART OF THE MATTER.

THE "MEOW" OF THAT PRIEST WAS HIGHLY SUSPICIOUS... AND NOT THE GODDESS BASTET! IN MY OPINION, THAT WAS REALLY A CAT!

RIGHT! THAT *PRECIOUS WORD* WAS ABSOLUTELY AN AUTHENTIC HOWL OF PAIN!

THERE'S NO DOUBT ABOUT IT: THOSE THREE ARE THE PIRATE CATS DISGUISED AS RODENTS!

WE'VE GOT TO UNMASK THEM!

BUT WE NEED PROOF! WITH THE FAVOR THEY ENJOY AT COURT, WE RUN THE RISK OF HAVING THE PHARAOH AND THE VIZIER AGAINST US!

YOU'RE A REGULAR SCAREDY CAT, GERONIMO!

~HUMPH!~

NO, G IS RIGHT! LET'S WATCH THEM FROM A DISTANCE! SOONER OR LATER, THEY'LL MAKE A FALSE STEP AND THEN WE'LL UNMASK THEM!

AT THE SAME TIME, IN ANOTHER WING OF THE PALACE...

YOU AND YOUR *BIG MOUTH!* YOU ALMOST GOT US DISCOVERED!

LUCKILY TERSILLA TRIMMED YOUR SAILS!✱

✱SHUT YOU UP!

SORRY, BUT WHEN I SAW GERONIMO, MY FUR BRISTLED IN FEAR!

ANYWAY, STILTON'S PRESENCE AT COURT IS A PROBLEM!

THOSE DUMMIES COULD SPOIL OUR PLANS!

DO YOU REALLY THINK SO?

OF COURSE! WHAT USUALLY HAPPENS WHEN GERONIMO STILTON AND HIS FRIENDS STEP INTO OUR PLANS?

THEY RUIN EVERYTHING!

NO FAIR! SHE ASKED ME THAT QUESTION!

MEOW DOWN✻, DADDY DEAR! KEEP AN EYE ON THEM AND TRY TO THINK OF A WAY TO GET RID OF THEM WITHOUT ANYONE SUSPECTING US!

✻ CALM DOWN

OKAY! IN THE MEANTIME, WHAT ARE YOU GOING TO DO?

I'M GOING TO CONCENTRATE ON RAT-KARUE: BY HOOK OR BY CROOK, THE SPHINX WILL HAVE THE FACE OF A FELINE!

THE FOLLOWING DAY, WE FOCUSED ON OUR TASKS, AND THERE WAS LITTLE TIME LEFT OVER FOR US TO INVESTIGATE...

WOE IS ME! I'M A JOURNALIST, NOT A WEAVER!

TESSITURA
THE CLOTHES WORN IN ANCIENT EGYPT WERE MOSTLY MADE OUT OF VERY FINE LINEN, ALMOST VOILE. THE FABRIC WAS MADE FROM THE FIBERS AND STEMS OF THE LINEN PLANT, WHICH WAS THEN TWISTED INTO YARN AND WOVEN ON A WOODEN LOOM.

YIKES! YOU'VE NIBBLED ON EVERYTHING! HOW CAN I SERVE IT TO THE PHARAOH?

YUM, YUM... THIS IS GOOD, TOO.

HEE, HEE, HEE!

IT'S SO NICE TO PLAY TOGETHER!

HA, HA, HA!

⇥BRRR⇤...JUST LOOKING AT THIS GODDESS BRINGS UP MY *SCAREDY-CAT FRIGHT!*

IT'LL BE HARD TO PUT A LONG HYMN ON A SINGLE PAPYRUS! EVEN MORE SO WITH HIEROGLYPHICS -- I DRAW VERY BADLY!

PAPYRUS IS A PLANT WITH A LONG STEM AND LEAVES THAT GROWS IN THE SWAMPS ALONG THE NILE RIVER. IT WAS USED PRIMARILY TO MAKE SHEETS FOR WRITING, WHICH WERE MADE BY SOAKING THE LEAVES IN WATER AND THEN DRYING THEM IN THE SUN.

I WONDER IF I SHOULD TRY TO GET INSPIRED BY THINKING OF SOMETHING ELSE?

I COULD THINK OF A TART OF SMOKED CHEESE... OR MAYBE OF SOMEONE SPECIAL!

I'VE GOT IT! I'LL PRETEND THE HYMN IS FOR BASTET, BUT IN REALITY I'LL DEDICATE IT TO... *PETUNIA!*

OH, NOBLE FELINE GODDESS, WHEN I LOOK UPON YOU, I THINK, "YOU HAVE EYES THE COLOR OF THE SKY AND A HEART FILLED WITH LOVE..."

MEANWHILE, EVEN TERSILLA HAD HER PAWS IN ACTION...

RAT-KARLIE, WE HAVE TO SPEAK! IT'S URGENT!

HORUS' BEAK! I'M RESTING!

34

YOUR REST CAN WAIT! BASTET IS VERY *DISPLEASED* WITH YOU!

-:GULP!-

THE MONUMENT MUST BE FINISHED WITH THE FACE OF A CAT! OTHERWISE THE GODDESS WILL STOP FAVORING YOU!

BUT, BUT... I CAN'T DO ANYTHING! THE PHARAOH DOESN'T REALLY WANT TO HEAR ANYTHING ABOUT THE FACE OF A CAT!

IF CHEPHREN IS THE OBSTACLE... THE GODDESS ORDERS YOU TO *ELIMINATE* HIM!

WHAAAAAT?

BASTET THINKS YOU'D BE A BETTER PHARAOH THAN HIM!

M-M-ME?

YOU HAVE A DAY TO THINK IT OVER, RAT-KARUE...

WAIT, RAT-SHEPSUT!

REBELLING AGAINST THE PHARAOH IS A RISKY THING TO DO. I COULD LOSE MY FUR!

WHAT ARE YOU WORRYING ABOUT? BASTET IS WITH YOU AND SO YOU'LL WIND UP WITH ALL OF EGYPT!

HMM... FIRST OF ALL, I WILL NEED TO IMPRISON CHEPHREN AND HIS FAMILY!

EASY! THE GODDESS ALREADY KNOWS HOW AND WHERE TO DO IT! LISTEN...

IN THE MEANTIME, WE WENT ON WITH OUR WORK...

⇥GRRR⇤!

!?

TAKE THIS TASTER AWAY! HE'S DEVOURING ALL OUR SUPPLIES!

⇥SLURP!⇤

BAM

HA, HA, HA, HA!

⇥OOF⇤... HOW LONG DOES IT TAKE?!? WHAT MILK PAP!✱

...

✱ HOW BORING!

THE EVENING OF THE GRAND FESTIVAL ARRIVED AND WE FINALLY SAW OUR DEAR FRIEND AGAIN...

RATTY-ATUM!

MY FRIENDS!

36

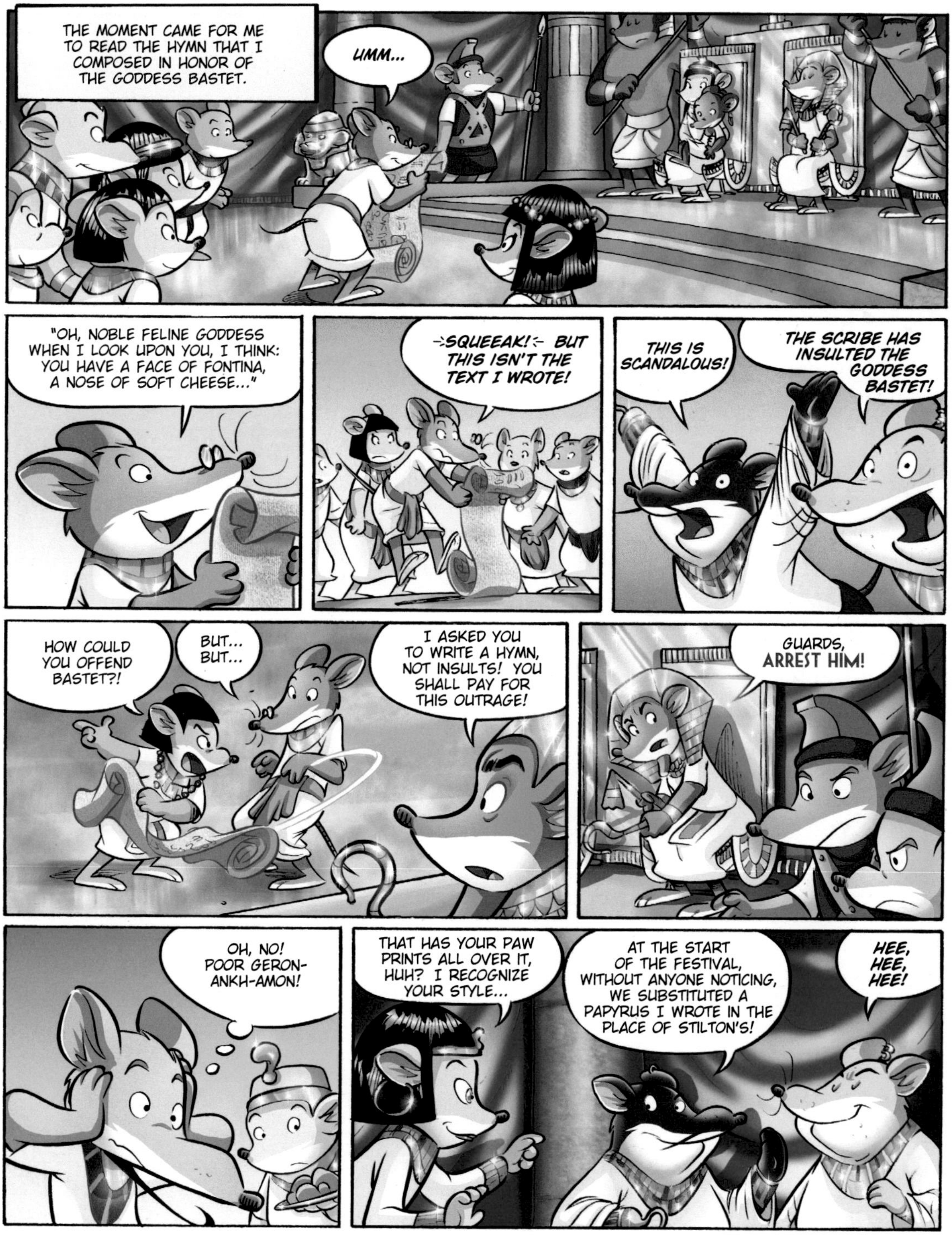
THE MOMENT CAME FOR ME TO READ THE HYMN THAT I COMPOSED IN HONOR OF THE GODDESS BASTET.
UMM...
"OH, NOBLE FELINE GODDESS WHEN I LOOK UPON YOU, I THINK: YOU HAVE A FACE OF FONTINA, A NOSE OF SOFT CHEESE..."
SQUEEAK! BUT THIS ISN'T THE TEXT I WROTE!
THIS IS SCANDALOUS!
THE SCRIBE HAS INSULTED THE GODDESS BASTET!
HOW COULD YOU OFFEND BASTET?!
BUT... BUT...
I ASKED YOU TO WRITE A HYMN, NOT INSULTS! YOU SHALL PAY FOR THIS OUTRAGE!
GUARDS, ARREST HIM!
OH, NO! POOR GERON-ANKH-AMON!
THAT HAS YOUR PAW PRINTS ALL OVER IT, HUH? I RECOGNIZE YOUR STYLE...
AT THE START OF THE FESTIVAL, WITHOUT ANYONE NOTICING, WE SUBSTITUTED A PAPYRUS I WROTE IN THE PLACE OF STILTON'S!
HEE, HEE, HEE!

DIVINE PHARAOH, I ASSURE YOU THAT IT WAS AN ERROR!

STOP!

!

IF YOU ARREST HIM, YOU'LL HAVE TO *ARREST ME, TOO!*

MY VERY DEAR NEPHEW!

AND ME, TOO!

AND ME, TOO!

AND ME, TOO! ONE RAT FOR ALL, ALL RATS FOR ONE!

SO BE IT! THE PRISON AIR WILL TAKE AWAY YOUR DESIRE TO INSULT THE GODS!

THEY DRAGGED US UNDER THE ROYAL PALACE AND LOCKED US UP IN A CELL.

WOULD YOU MIND TELLING ME WHAT YOU HAD IN MIND WHEN YOU WROTE THOSE WORDS?

HOW MANY TIMES DO I HAVE TO KEEP SAYING IT, I DIDN'T WRITE THAT!

THEN WHO COULD IT HAVE BEEN?

≈TSK!≈

MAYBE YOU WERE THE VICTIM OF THE PIRATE CATS' TRAP!

THAT'S RIGHT!

BUT WE CAN'T PROVE IT! LET'S TRY TO FIND A WAY TO GET OUT OF THIS CELL, INSTEAD!

MAYBE TRAP COULD EAT UP THE PRISON WALLS!

YOU'RE SO FUNNY, COUSIN!

LET'S FEEL THE WALLS! THERE COULD BE A *SECRET PASSAGE*!

KNOCK KNOCK

DON'T DELUDE YOURSELF, *YOU STUPID SQUEAKERS!* YOU'LL NEVER GET OUT OF THIS HOLE!

?!?

THE DANCER? THE PRIESTS?

FINALLY WE MEET! YOU MUST BE...

TERSILLA OF CATATONIA, DAUGHTER OF CATARDONE III!

THE PIRATE CATS... ~BRRR!~

I WANT YOU TO KNOW THAT BY TOMORROW, *HISTORY* WILL HAVE CHANGED... IN FAVOR OF CATS, OBVIOUSLY!

DURING HIS ANNUAL JOURNEY DOWN THE NILE, CHEPHREN WILL HAVE AN UNPLEASANT SURPRISE!

WH-WHAT DO YOU MEAN?

THAT THE PHARAOH WILL BE IMPRISONED BY RAT-KARUE AND FORCED TO SURRENDER HIS REIGN TO THE VIZIER!

THE VIZIER...
A TRAITOR?

IMPOSSIBLE!

OH, BUT HE IS! ALL I HAD TO DO TO CONVINCE HIM WAS PROMISE HIM THE TITLE OF PHARAOH!

RIGHT!

YOU'LL NEVER MANAGE TO IMPRISON THE PHARAOH!

IT WAS EASY WITH YOU, MOUSE!

MOLDY MOZZARELLA! WAS IT YOU WHO SUBSTITUTED THE PAPYRUS?!?

NOT TO BOAST...!

NOW I UNDERSTAND! WITH CHEPHREN OUT OF THE WAY, YOU'LL BE ABLE TO GIVE THE SPHINX THE FACE OF A CAT!

YOU GOT IT, *SWEETIE!* THAT WAY WE'LL BECOME POWERFUL AND FAMOUS...

GOODBYE, RATLINGS! I HOPE YOU LIKE YOUR CELL, BECAUSE YOUR ONLY CHANCE OF LEAVING IT...

...WILL BE IF SOME ARCHAEOLOGIST STUMBLES UPON YOU IN A FEW MILLENNIA!

SLAM

WHAT WICKED RATS!

LET'S LOOK FOR A WAY TO GET OUT! WE PROMISED VON VOLT THAT WE'D STOP THE PIRATE CATS AND WE'RE GOING TO SUCCEED!

WE SPENT THE REST OF THE NIGHT LOOKING FOR A WAY TO ESCAPE...

KNOCK
KNOCK
KNOCK

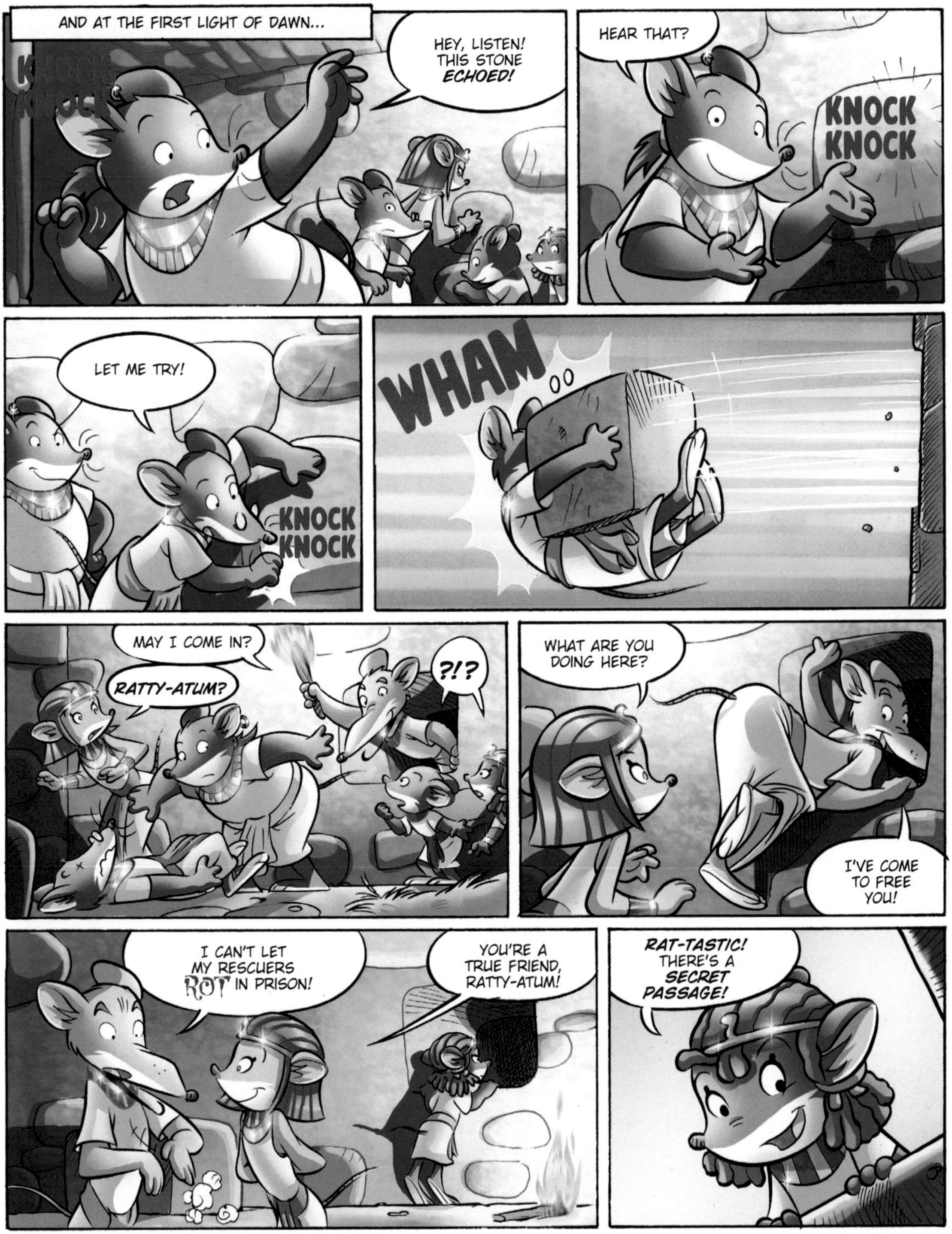
AND AT THE FIRST LIGHT OF DAWN...
KNOCK KNOCK
HEY, LISTEN! THIS STONE ECHOED!
HEAR THAT?
KNOCK KNOCK
LET ME TRY!
KNOCK KNOCK
WHAM
MAY I COME IN?
RATTY-ATUM?
?!?
WHAT ARE YOU DOING HERE?
I'VE COME TO FREE YOU!
I CAN'T LET MY RESCUERS ROT IN PRISON!
YOU'RE A TRUE FRIEND, RATTY-ATUM!
RAT-TASTIC! THERE'S A SECRET PASSAGE!

OH, YES, THE PALACE UNDERGROUND IS FULL OF THEM! CHEPHREN'S ANCESTORS HAD THEM BUILT SO THEY COULD ESCAPE AT ANY MOMENT!

THE GODS REALLY WANTED ME TO BE THE ONE IN CHARGE OF LAST YEAR'S RESTORATION WORK!

AND... WHERE DOES THIS PASSAGE GO?

AH, YOU'RE AWAKE NOW, COUSIN!

IT COMES OUT ON THE BANKS OF THE NILE!

THE NILE?

RATTY-ATUM, YOU'VE GOT TO LISTEN TO US... THE PHARAOH IS IN GRAVE DANGER!

~GULP!~

IN SHORT, WE TOLD OUR FRIEND ABOUT THE PIRATE CATS' PLAN...

...LEAVING OUT ONLY THE DETAIL OF TIME TRAVEL.

CATS! I MUST RUN AND SAVE THE PHARAOH!

WE'LL COME, TOO!

MOLDY MOZZARELLA! I'M AFRAID OF TIGHT SPACES!

WATCH YOUR HEADS! THE TUNNEL GETS EVEN NARROWER FARTHER ALONG!

MEANWHILE, CHEPHREN'S SHIP WAS TRAVELING ALONG THE NILE TOWARDS GIZA, THE FIRST STAGE OF A JOURNEY THAT WOULD TAKE THE PHARAOH AND HIS FAMILY TO THE MOUTH OF THE RIVER AT THE MEDITERRANEAN SEA...

THE NILE IS THE LONGEST RIVER IN THE WORLD: ITS COURSE IS SOME 4,145 MILES LONG (INCLUDING ITS FIRST BRANCH, THE NILE KAGERA), ENDING AT THE MEDITERRANEAN SEA. IN ANTIQUITY, ITS PERIODIC FLOODS MADE THE FIELDS FERTILE SINCE THEY DEPOSITED PRECIOUS MUD SILT ONTO THE GROUND.

WHAT'S GOING ON, MICERINO? YOU'VE BEEN SAD EVER SINCE YESTERDAY EVENING! DO YOU MISS YOUR FRIENDS?

YES, MAMA...

MICERINO, ONE DAY YOU WILL REIGN OVER EVERYTHING IN MY PLACE! YOU MUST LEARN THAT THE PHARAOH CANNOT ALLOW THE GODS TO BE INSULTED!

EXACTLY, CHEPHREN! SO WHY DO YOU CONTINUE TO OPPOSE THE WILL OF BASTET!

RAT-KARUE, HOW DARE YOU ADDRESS ME IN THAT TONE?

I DARE BECAUSE BASTET GAVE ME THE RIGHT TO DO SO!

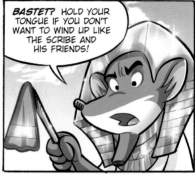

BASTET? HOLD YOUR TONGUE IF YOU DON'T WANT TO WIND UP LIKE THE SCRIBE AND HIS FRIENDS!

PRIESTS, TELL HIM WHOSE SIDE THE GODDESS IS ON!

ON THAT OF RAT-KARUE... DEAREST EX-PHARAOH!

HEE, HEE, HEE...

WHAT ARE THESE WORDS?

GUARDS, ARREST THE ROYAL FAMILY!

BUT--BUT--

TREASON! ALL OF EGYPT WILL REBEL AGAINST THIS PLOT!

YOU'RE WASTING YOUR BREATH, CHEPHREN... EGYPT WILL ONLY KNOW THAT YOU AND YOUR FAMILY HAD AN ACCIDENT DURING THE TRIP!

EVEN WHEN YOU'RE FAVORED BY THE GODS, IT'S NOT WISE TO SWIM IN A RIVER INFESTED WITH CROCODILES...

~GRRR~... *SCOUNDRELS!*

NOT FAR AWAY...

WE'VE GOT TO SAIL *FASTER!*

WHAT CAN WE DO?

RIGHT...THIS BOAT IS TOO SLOW!

WE CAN JUMP INTO THE WATER AND PUSH THE BOAT!

WHAT ARE YOU SAYING? THAT'S TOO HARD -- WE CAN'T DO IT!

YOU'RE A REGULAR CHEESE-HEAD! ALL YOU HAVE TO DO IS GRAB THE SHIP AND MOVE YOUR LEGS A BIT!

HMM...

COME ON! IT'S THE ONLY WAY TO GO FASTER!

A LITTLE LATER...

~PUFF, PANT...~ I CAN'T DO IT ANYMORE!

BUT I'M DOING IT ALL MYSELF!

COME ON, COUSIN, APPLY SOME GRIT! LEARN FROM THOSE CROCODILES!

HUH?

CROCODILES?!?

AAHHHHRGGHHH!

ZOOOOMMM

YES, NOW THAT'S GOING FAST!

HEE, HEE, HEE... IT'S LIKE WE'RE IN A MOTORBOAT.

OVER THERE! THAT'S CHEPHREN'S SHIP!

PERFECT! NOW YOU CAN EVEN SLOW DOWN!

HEY! I SAID YOU COULD SLOW DO--

SWIISH

?

!

CRAASH

--WN?!?

WHAT WAS THAT CRASH?

COULD IT HAVE BEEN A CRASH OF **THUNDER?**

⇥ARGH!⇤

⇥SQUEAK!⇤

BOING

BOING

IT'S RAINING RATS!

THE SCRIBE AND THE TASTER?

⇥GULP!⇤ GERONIMO STILTON!

WE'RE HERE, TOO, TRAITORS!

RATTY-ATUM?!?

GUARDS! ARREST THEM! ARREST THEM ALL!

AT YOUR COMMAND!

SLAMM

!

WHOOOSHH

SLAMM

OWOWOWOW!

IT LOOKS TO ME LIKE STILTON HAS RUINED OUR PLANS ONCE AGAIN!

-»HUMPH«-... WHICH DO YOU PREFER? PRISON OR WATER?

PRISON!

WATER!

SORRY, DADDY DEAR, BUT THIS TIME BONZO'S RIGHT!

!

THUMP

I HATE WAAAATER!

SPLASH

YOU WON, RATS IN BOOTS! BUT WE'LL SEE EACH OTHER AGAIN SOON -- I SWEAR IT BY THE WORD OF TERSILLA!

THEY ALWAYS MANAGE TO SLIP AWAY!

RIGHT, BUT I'LL BET WE'LL MEET THEM AGAIN!

THANKS, RATTY-ATUM, YOU SAVED ME! HOW DID YOU KNOW THAT--

I'LL EXPLAIN EVERYTHING TO YOU! YOU WON'T BELIEVE YOUR EARS!

WELL, WHERE DID THE TRAITOROUS VIZIER DISAPPEAR?

-»SIGH!«-

I SPOTTED HIM HIDING AMONG THE EXTRA FRUIT!

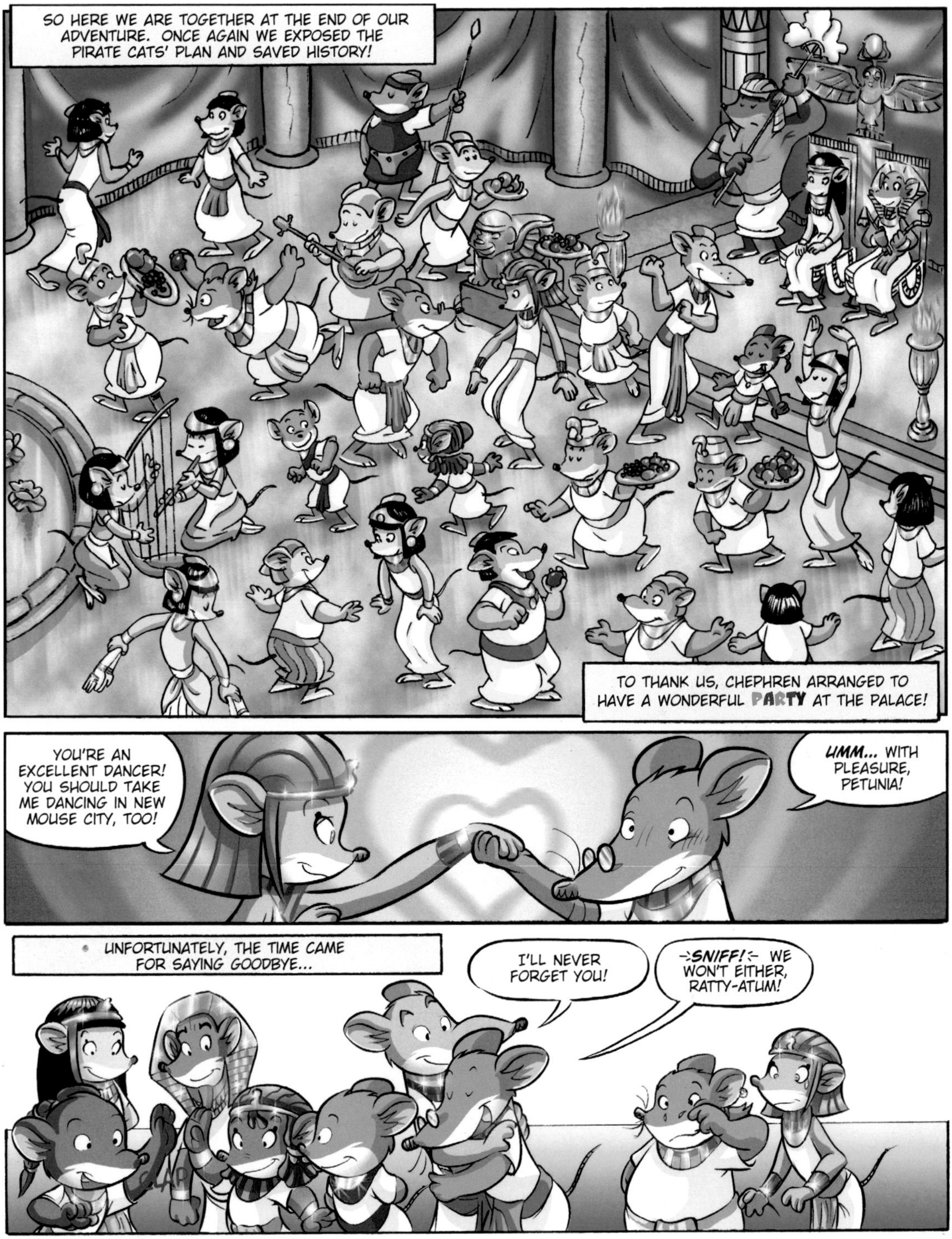
SO HERE WE ARE TOGETHER AT THE END OF OUR ADVENTURE. ONCE AGAIN WE EXPOSED THE PIRATE CATS' PLAN AND SAVED HISTORY!
TO THANK US, CHEPHREN ARRANGED TO HAVE A WONDERFUL PARTY AT THE PALACE!
YOU'RE AN EXCELLENT DANCER! YOU SHOULD TAKE ME DANCING IN NEW MOUSE CITY, TOO!
UMM... WITH PLEASURE, PETUNIA!
UNFORTUNATELY, THE TIME CAME FOR SAYING GOODBYE...
I'LL NEVER FORGET YOU!
SNIFF! WE WON'T EITHER, RATTY-ATUM!

IN NEW MOUSE CITY, A FRIEND WAS WAITING TO TOAST US WITH CHEESE MOUSSE!

POP

PROFESSOR VON VOLT!

FRIENDS!

COME ON, TELL ME EVERYTHING!

YOUR SUSPICIONS WERE CORRECT: THE CATS' GOAL REALLY WAS THE SPHINX!

THEY WANTED TO GIVE IT THE FACE OF A CAT!

RIGHT, BUT THANKS TO US, IT STILL HAS THE APPEARANCE TODAY THAT WE ALL KNOW!

THE FACE OF THE PHARAOH CHEPHREN!

ALTHOUGH, IF YOU LOOK HARD... YUM, YUM... THE FACE OF THE SPHINX LOOKS A LITTLE FAMILIAR!

FAMILIAR?

YES, IF THE SPHINX HAD A PAIR OF GLASSES, IT WOULD LOOK A LOT LIKE YOU, COUSIN!

?

D-D-DO YOU REALLY THINK SO?

HA, HA, HA!

OF COURSE NOT, I WAS JUST KIDDING!

SMACK

SQUEEEAK!

HA, HA, HA!

MY DEAR RODENT FRIENDS, FAREWELL UNTIL THE NEXT ADVENTURE... ANOTHER WHISKERFUL OF AN ADVENTURE WRITTEN BY STILTON...

Geronimo Stilton!

Watch Out For
PAPERCUTZ

You know, I'm really jealous of Geronimo Stilton! You see, both Geronimo and I are Editors-in-Chief. He edits the Rodent's Gazette, the most famouse paper on Mouse Island, and I edit Papercutz graphic novels, the most famous graphic novels published at 160 Broadway, on Manhattan Island. But Geronimo can do something I can't do – he can travel through time!

Wow! If I could travel through time, none of our graphic novels would ever be late! Not that Stefan Petrucha, Sarah Kinney, and Sho Murase are ever late writing or drawing our NANCY DREW DIARIES graphic novels, but I'm sure they'd all love to take a break and travel back in time to witness some of history's most famous unsolved mysteries.

Stefan Petrucha and Paulo Henrique would probably want to stop time, catch their breath from writing and drawing THE POWER RANGERS graphic novels, and get together to create a movie, with Stefan writing and directing and Paulo starring and performing the score.

Greg Farshtey would secretly love to take a little time off from writing every LEGO® NINJAGO story Papercutz ever published, to actually have time to play with the amazing constructible action figures from LEGO that star in all his stories.

Of course, if you're a real comicbook fan like me, you couldn't resist going back in time and picking up the original CLASSICS ILLUSTRATED and TALES FROM THE CRYPT comicbooks right off the newsstands for only 15 cents or 10 cents each. Today the comics are worth a whole lot more! Who knows, maybe one day our Papercutz CLASSICS ILLUSTRATED and TALES FROM THE CRYPT graphic novels will be worth a small fortune too?

Well, I may not be able to travel through time, but I can show you a little bit of the future! On the following pages we have a special sneak preview of GERONIMO STILTON #3 "The Coliseum Con." It's the next exciting GERONIMO STILTON graphic novel from Papercutz, and it's available now at booksellers everywhere. In the meantime, visit me at www.papercutz.com and tell us what you think of this graphic novel. We really want to hear from you, and I hope you post your comments on our Papercutz Blog for all your fellow Geronimo Stilton fans to see! Of course, there's always lots of fun awaiting you at www.geronimostilton.com, but I bet you already knew that!

Until next time, here's wishing Professor Von Volt can whip up a time machine that will help me get into the Papercutz offices before Associate Editor Mike Petranek!

Thanks,

Jim

STAY IN TOUCH!

EMAIL: salicrup@papercutz.com
WEB: www.papercutz.com
TWITTER: @papercutzgn
FACEBOOK: PAPERCUTZGRAPHICNOVELS
FAN MAIL: Papercutz, 160 Broadway, Suite 700,
                  East Wing, New York, NY 10038

Caricature of Jim by Steve Brodner drawn at the MoCCA Art Fest.

Special Preview of GERONIMO STILTON Graphic Novel #3 – "The Coliseum Con"!

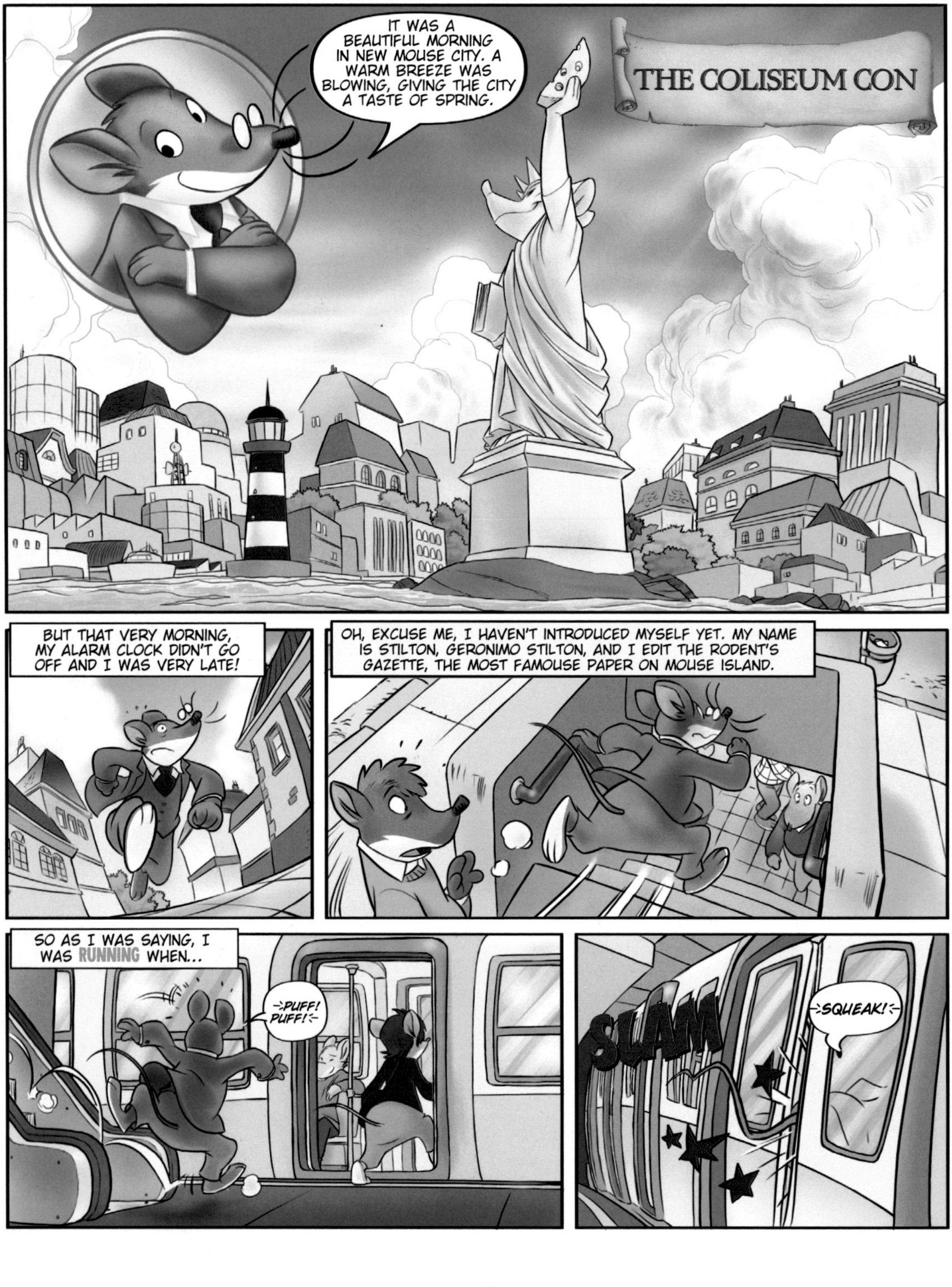

IT WAS A BEAUTIFUL MORNING IN NEW MOUSE CITY. A WARM BREEZE WAS BLOWING, GIVING THE CITY A TASTE OF SPRING.
THE COLISEUM CON
BUT THAT VERY MORNING, MY ALARM CLOCK DIDN'T GO OFF AND I WAS VERY LATE!
OH, EXCUSE ME, I HAVEN'T INTRODUCED MYSELF YET. MY NAME IS STILTON, GERONIMO STILTON, AND I EDIT THE RODENT'S GAZETTE, THE MOST FAMOUSE PAPER ON MOUSE ISLAND.
SO AS I WAS SAYING, I WAS RUNNING WHEN...
PUFF! PUFF!
SLAM
SQUEAK!

~:SQUEAK!:~
MY POOR TAIL!

~:SQUEEAK!:~
MY POOR PAW!

~:SQUEEEAK!:~
MY POOR NOSE!

BAM

OOPS!

I FINALLY GOT TO THE OFFICE, BUT MY PROBLEMS WEREN'T OVER...

GERONIMO, THERE'S A VERY IMPORTANT VISITOR FOR YOU!

IT WAS THE FAMOUS OPERA SINGER RATIDO DOMINGO!

AH, GOOD MORNING, DR. STILTON!

UM...GOOD MORNING!

I INTEND TO PUBLISH MY BIOGRAPHY AND I WANT YOU TO **WRITE IT!**

M-ME?

I GREATLY ADMIRE YOUR BOOKS AND I KNOW THAT YOU'LL BE ABLE TO FIND THE RIGHT WORDS TO DESCRIBE MY ART! LISTEN...

BE GONE, OH RAT! FADE AWAY, MOZZARELLA! AT DAWN, I SHALL SQUEAK...!

?!?

?!?

SQUITTIRO0000o

?!?

?!?

?!?

SO/CRASH CRASH CRASH

ITTIRO0000oo

SO WHAT DO YOU SAY, MR. STILTON?

CRASH

?!?

I GOT RID OF RATIDO BY PROMISING TO THINK ABOUT HIS IDEA AND STARTED WORK-ING, BUT I WAS IMMEDIATELY INTERRUPTED...

WHO COULD THAT BE?

RING RING RING

GERONIMO!

-SQUEEAK!-

IT WAS MY GRANDFATHER, WILLIAM SHORTPAWS, AKA "CHEAP MOUSE WILLY"...

UM..HELLO, GRANDPA!

WAKE UP!

HAVE YOU READ THE THE DAILY RAT?

ACTUALLY, THAT'S SALLY RATMOUSEN'S PAPER. MINE'S CALLED--

I KNOW PERFECTLY WELL WHAT THE PAPER I FOUNDED IS CALLED!

THAT RAT'S PAPER HAS AN ARTICLE ON RATIDO DOMINGO'S CONCERT, BUT THERE'S NOTHING ABOUT IT IN THE RODENT'S GAZETTE!

RATIDO? THAT'S ODD... HE WAS HERE A LITTLE WHILE AGO!

WHAT? AND YOU DIDN'T INTERVIEW HIM?

WHAT DO YOU DO IN YOUR OFFICE, SLEEP? WAKE UUUP!

WAKE UUUP!!!

WAKE UUUUP!

?!?

?!?

WAKE UUUUP!!!

CRASH

CRASH

CRASH

GRANDSON? ARE YOU STILL THERE? WHAT ARE YOU DOING... ARE YOU REALLY ASLEEP?

AFTER A DAY LIKE THAT, I DIDN'T WANT TO DO ANYTHING BESIDES GO HOME AND NIBBLE ON SOME CHEESE AND CRACKERS...

INSTEAD...

ROTTEN ROQUEFORT! THE REFRIGERATOR'S EMPTY!

~SIGH!~

DEAR COUSIN, I WAS PASSING THROUGH AND GOT HUNGRY! NEXT TIME COULD YOU BUY SOME FRESH MOZZARELLA, TOO?

THANKS! TRAP

I WAS ABOUT TO GO LOOK FOR A STORE THAT WAS OPEN, WHEN...

RRRIIINGG RRRIIINNGG

THE TELEPHONE?

WHO KNOWS WHO THAT IS? LET'S HOPE IT'S NOT SOMEONE ELSE WHO WANTS TO SCREAM IN MY EAR!

BRIIIPPP

H-HELLO?

HELLO, GERONIMO? IT'S **AMPY VON VOLT!**

AH, GOOD EVENING, PROFESSOR!

SORRY TO DISTURB YOU, BUT YOU MUST COME TO MY LABORATORY RIGHT AWAY!

NOW? TO TELL THE TRUTH, I--

IT'S AN EMERGENCY! THE PIRATE CATS HAVE GONE INTO ACTION!

THE P-P-PIRATE CATS?!?

YES! THE TEMPOGRAPH, THE DEVICE I INVENTED TO MONITOR HISTORY, SHOWS THAT THEY'RE TRAVELLING INTO THE PAST!

Don't miss GERONIMO STILTON
Graphic Novel #3 – "The Coliseum Con"

OKAY, I'LL TAKE YOU INTO MY SERVICE! YOUR ARRIVAL AND THE FAVOR OF BASTET WILL BE A BLESSING FOR ALL OF EGYPT!

YOU WON'T REGRET IT, OH MOST ILLUSTRIOUS VIZIER!

-:SOB!:- I PREDICT HARD TIMES FOR MY TAIL!

OH, BUT HE IS! ALL I HAD TO DO TO CONVVNCE HIM WAS PROMISE HIM THE TITLE OF PHARAOH!

RIGHT!

THE PIRATE CATS TRAVEL TO THE PAST ON THE CATJET SO THAT THEY CAN CHANGE HISTORY AND BECOME RICH AND FAMOUSE. BUT GERONIMO AND THE STILTON FAMILY ALWAYS MANAGE TO UNMASK THEM!

CATJET

HMM... HOW CAN I BE SURE THIS ISN'T SOME KIND OF **TRICK?**

IF YOU DON'T BELIEVE US, MOST ILLUSTRIOUS VIZIER, TRY IT YOURSELF!

YES, MOST ILLUSTRIOUS VIZIER, JUST TREAD ON HIS TAIL!

HEY... JUST A MINUTE!